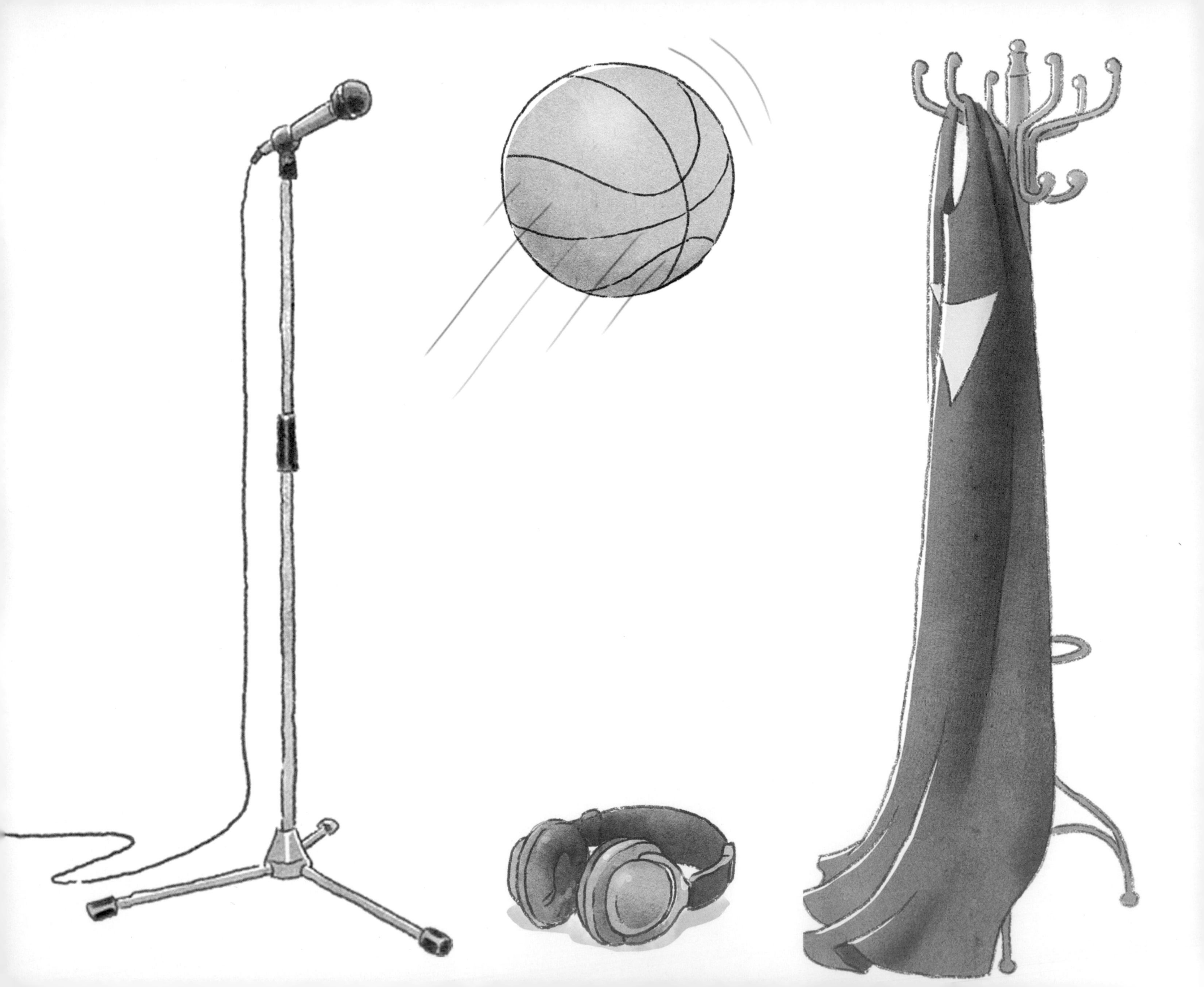

This book is inspired by and dedicated to some of the many amazing men who have touched our lives closely and from afar with their own special brand of brilliance. We thank you, honor you, and salute you. We are all better that you walk with victorious swagger as Kings, supremely beside us:

Warren T. Drummond / Lawrence Christmas / John W. Bynum / John Drummond / Rodney Michael King / James P. Newson / Elroy Pinks / Sifu Earl White / Don Bartlow / CDR Bobby E. Brown, Jr.

Chris Rock
Reggie Hudlin
Earvin "Magic" Johnson
Taj Gibson
Stephen Curry
Rep. John Lewis
Dikembe Mutombo
Warwick Dunn
John Singleton
Spike Lee
Floyd Norman
Nate Parker
Todd B. Williams
Sidney Poitier

Nas
Kendrick Lamar
J. Cole
DeRay Mckesson
Steve Harvey
Jesse Williams
Ta-Nehisi Coates
Marshawn Lynch
Henry "Hank" Aaron
Neil deGrasse Tyson
Darin Atwater
John Legend
Tim King
Denzel Washington

Samuel L. Jackson
Colin L. Powell
Eric Holder
Willie Mays
Cory Booker
Tony Elumelu
Lester Holt
Henry Louis Gates, Jr.
Wendell Pierce
Harry Belafonte
Bishop Charles E. Blake
Stevie Wonder
Blair Underwood
Muhammad Ali

and

President Barack H. Obama
44th President of the United States of America

For in your depths, 'yond passion's query
hopes pressed strong within you rise;
Truth unshackles silent fury
as beauty even deeper lies.
A princely poise,
Proud,
Dignity grand;
If only your grace
were of every man.

—Excerpt from "A Man Supreme"
by Betty K. Bynum

"I came here to plead with you…
Believe in yourself and believe that you are somebody.
Nobody else can do this for you…
Don't let anybody take your manhood.
Somebody told a lie one day…
But I want to get the language right… I want to get the language
so right that everybody here will cry out…
'Yes, I'm Black. I'm proud of it.
I'm Black and beautiful'."

—Selected words from a speech by
Dr. Martin Luther King, Jr.

Author: Joshua B. Drummond Author/Art Director/Editor: Betty K. Bynum Design/Type and Page Layouts: Betty K. Bynum and Warren T. Drummond
Graphic Designer: Brian Boehm Creative Consultant: Lawrence Christmas
ISBN Hardback: 978-0-692-55532-3 Library of Congress Control Number [LCCN]: 2016903050

First Edition.
Printed in China. 14 13 12 11 10 09 1 2 3 4 5 6 7 8 9 10

BRILLIANT

bril-liant (bril yant) adjective.

1. Full of light; shining. 2. Glorious, magnificent. 3. superb; wonderful. 4. marked by unusual and impressive intellectual acuteness. Remarkable. Extraordinary. Exceptional clarity and agility of intellect or invention. Having or showing great intelligence, talent, quality. 5. a precious gem, especially a diamond in any various forms with numerous facets. Radiant. Grand. Illustrious. Distinguished. Splendid.

To shine.

#Bb Bbrilliant #Bb Bbrilliant #Bb Bbrilliant #Bb Bbrilliant

I'm A
Brilliant
Little
Black
Boy!
Written by
Joshua B. Drummond
and
Betty K. Bynum
Illustrated by
Brian McGee

My mom says that stars shine
bright in the night,
So the night can be filled
with sparkles of light!

She said that "BRILLIANT"
is the word to describe the shine
of the stars that make us smile.

"Like you, when I wake
to see you every day!
You are like a star
that lights everything
in every way;

'Cause your smile
shines bright, both night
and day."

I say,
"You mean like a shiny,
brand new toy?
Well, I must be a BRILLIANT
little Black boy!"

"So, be brilliant"
then she kissed my face.

I'll sleep... and be
ALL THAT when I wake!

Adventure Day

at school is my favorite day,
"Ooooo weeeee!"
We dress as characters we like
and some we'd like to be.

My hand raised high to know
the answer,
"Call on me, please, call on me!"
I'm happy if she calls my name,
(If not, I'll be fine just the same).

A fireman, cowboy and chef—
and SIX girls like ballet!

Teacher asks me,
"Joshua, what does your
PIRATE say?"
I yell, "Land ho!" and
"Ships Ahoy!"
Now, I'm a SMART little
Black boy!

I read books in our library
that show our earth's a mystery.

Oceans filled with fish so deep,
some fish we'll never, ever see!

Class experiments can show
how huge volcanoes overflow.
They bubble deep from way below;
"Stand back!" I say,
"It's going to blow!"

My classmates jump…
and cheer…
and then…
WHOOOOSSSHHH!!!
The lava is safe, it's just pretend.

I'm inventive!
(but it's really not so scientific)
There're mighty things I CAN DO,
I believe—but first I THINK it!

Art class is really cool!
What you create—
you get to take it!
You never know exactly
what you're making
'til you make it.

Colors of the rainbow,
Brushes of different size;
You start one way, but when you
finish up...
it's a SURPRISE!

What I paint is what I dream:
Houses made of cookies!
Pools of ice cream!
Pet dinosaurs and flying
cars to race!
Zooming rocket ships!
Dragon battles in space!

You're free to paint your dreams—
not to prove that
you're the smartest.
Pencils, crayons, paper, paint
just draw—and WOW!
You're an artist!

A paint brush can be much better
than any kind of toy;
with pencils, crayons,
paper, paint...
I'm an ARTISTIC little Black Boy!

Some days, I like
to speak my mind,
I do it best with poetry time!
Hear my life, through spoken word,
my voice lifts like wings of a bird!
When I speak rhymes, then I am heard.
My rhymes fly free like flying birds,
instead, the sky's painted with words!
IMAGINATION! That's the key!
It's inside us, invisibly.
Imagination's what I use,
'cause it feels like struttin'
in new shoes!
It takes me places far and new,
it lets me share my rhymes with you!
Imagination lets me see
in words,
what's deep inside of me.
All I do is just believe...
then, WOW! The possibilities!

It's way cool fun, when words just come,
I spin my words to the rhythm!
Before school and even lunch time
my friends and I just rhyme and rhyme.
"BOOF BOOF, BOOM BOOM"
line after line,
we free-flow cool words all the time.
Beats, syllables,
words, thoughts and rhyme...
Oh yea, oh yea... it's poetry time!
Beats, syllables,words,
thoughts and rhyme!
...HIP-HOP, don't stop...
it's poetry time!

"Hip-Hop, don't stop!"

Jump off the table!
Jump off the chair!
My red cape flying in the air!
A SUPERHERO jumps the wall!
In my red cape—I'm ten feet tall!
The Superhero of my neighborhood.
My powers are for super-good!

Is Elroy's cat stuck in a tree?
Not for long! My cape and me
will get him free.
Climb up… hold tight…
slide down little cat!
"Hey, Josh! How'd you even
THINK to do THAT?!"

People laugh, clap
and cheer with joy,
"Now, that's a clever little boy!"
My cape and me!
Yep, now 'ya know,
just call me,
JOSH the SUPERHERO!

It does not matter the size I am,
I still make all the
bad guys SCRAM!
Big Cory bullied little Zack,
but I stand by my friend,
I've got his back.

Big Cory thinks he's big and tough,
but I told him,
"Stop! That's enough!"

No red cape's needed
to do what's right.

NO BULLIES HERE!

Just FRIENDS... *no fights!*

I help my Mom with chores
each day,
"Here's your allowance,"
she will say.
I start to put it in my can,
Then think…
"I'll open a lemonade stand!"

I buy lemons and honey,
add water and get cups,
I stir it all together fast,
to sweeten it up.
And candy bars—I get a whole box,
And sell them too
'cause kids love them a lot.

"LEMONADE FOR SALE!,"
I shout and yell.
"And candy, too!
Right here for you!"

I say, "THANK YOU!"
and "HAVE A NICE DAY!"
Look how much money
that I've made!

And MY customers SMILE,
so I do enjoy,
being a BUSINESS-OWNING
little Black Boy!

At the BARBERSHOP!
I wait my turn for the BIG chair.
I look at my lumpy, curly,
shiny, thick black hair.

"A haircut, Mr. Roy.
And please, buzz-cut it
so it's smooth."
"Alright, little man,
I'll take your word
and smooth it, just for you."

The clippers buzz, and buzz…
and when
My hair's all lined-up,
the chair spins.

He takes a jar with something in it,
"It's tonic—it'll sting,
but just for a minute.
Now, look and see," says Mr. Roy.
"Hmmm…
I'm a HANDSOME little Black Boy!"

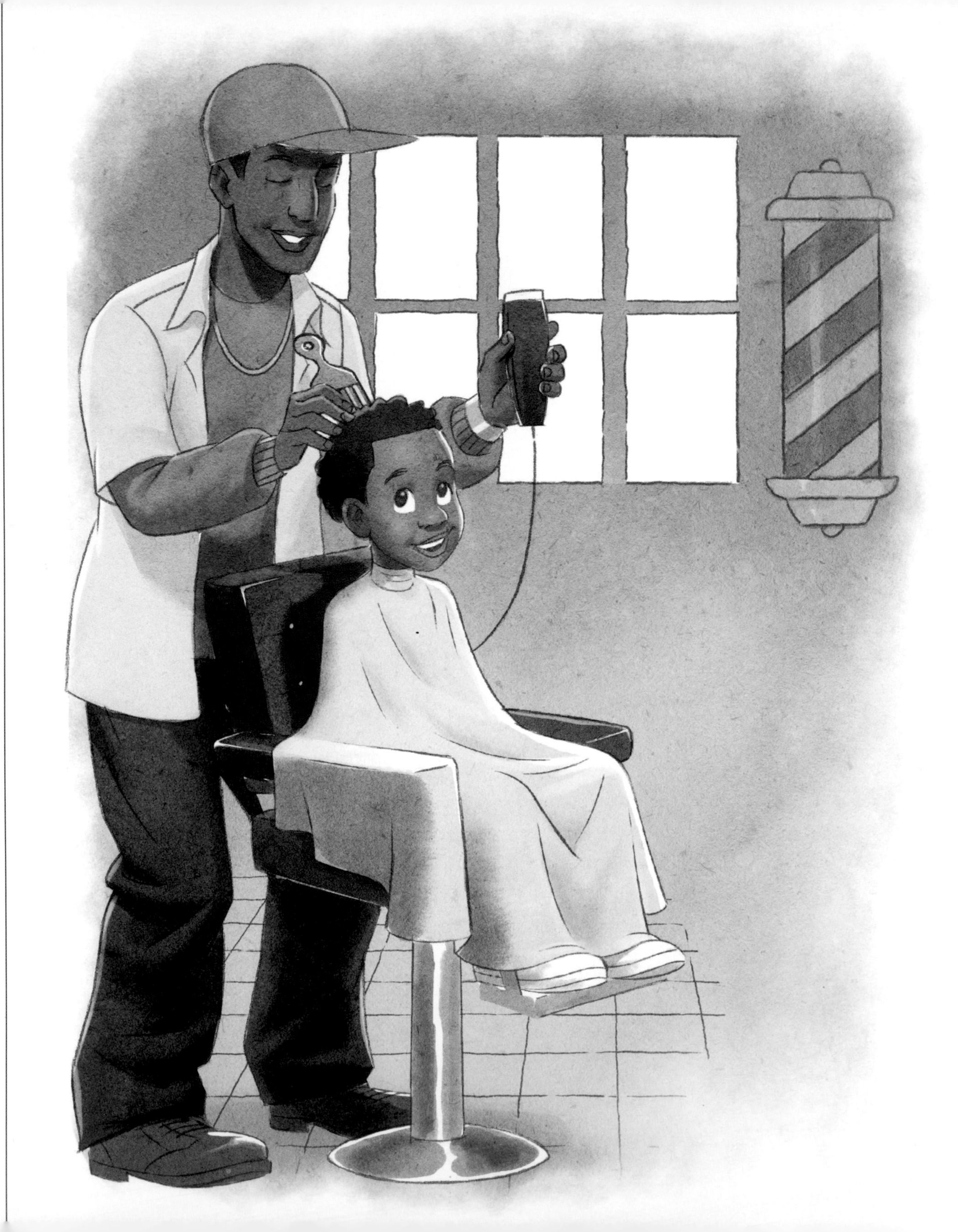

TON

Ball through the hoop!

BASKETBALL!

BASKETBALL!

BAS…KET…BALL!!!
Yep! That's our sport!
We run, bounce and dribble
all over the court!
Run, jump, shoot…
Ball through the hoop!
Win or lose, lose or win,
We all have fun, 'cause we all join in.

Basketball! Oh, yea!
We'll play all day, 'cause it's OUR GAME!
The court gives us a kind of freedom
I just can't explain.
If I could grab the wind
and ride on clouds
that never let me fall…
THAT'S how it feels when
I am happy playing basketball!

Just show your confidence,
That's all that matters since,
it's BASKETBALL! And it's OUR GAME!
Nothing matters when we play,
we're all one TEAM
and glad we came to play… to PLAY!
Sometimes at night,
sometimes ALL DAY.
We LOVE to play—and yes!
OH, YES!…we're HAPPY to be in it,
But if you ask me, I'll confess—
WE'RE STILL in it to WIN IT!

My friends and I become
an ARMY,
Toy swords and shields,
now no one harms me.

The sun is hot, supplies are heavy,
But we won't stop
'til our fort is ready.

My friends are here, I'm not alone
Bound to no rules, we have our own.
These are MY BOYS!
And we're TEAM PROUD!
We're kings of the park!
(no parents allowed.)

Cut, paste, tape, hammer—
the signs are hung!
"Good job, guys! The fort is done!"

Who leads others to succeed?
I'm a LEADER, yep, that's ME!

Park rd.

NO
PARENTS
ALLOWED

As the sun begins to set,
we count the FIREFLIES we get!
We close them tight
in glass jars, so…
we watch them buzz,
light up and glow.

"They should be free,
I'll let them go" but then…
My friends say, "No!
Let's keep them in!"
I ask them,
"Would you like being
stuck in a JAR??
When you'd really like
to FLY away…far??!
Would you like being stuck,
like THIS??"
"No," said Greg. "No," said Malik.
"No," said Zack, Cory and Chris.
David, John, Steve and Elroy,
All seemed to pout and be annoyed.

"Let's let them go,
let's let them out,
They give us days to think about;
They'll multiply, and then there'll be
MORE fireflies—
much more than these
right near our fort, under the trees.
Don't keep them in,
they'll come again.
Tomorrow—they'll come
look for you,
and we'll see them
tomorrow, too!"

They say, "Okay," 'cause
they're MY BOYS!
They all agree, "It's not nice
to destroy."
I lift the lid and shout command:
"Move out soldiers! Let's deploy!"
And I say,
I'm a KIND little Black Boy!"

When we are having fun outside
the daylight-time goes quickly by.

Street lights come ON!…
that warn and show,

"UH OH!!"

"OH, SNAP!!"

"It's time to *G-o-o-o-o-o!*"

We start to dash!

We say, "SO LONG!"

My Daddy's voice comes loud and strong:

"JOSHUA-*A-AAhhhhhh!*

Come in the house,
you've been out too long!"

There're things that
I can only hope
to see with my small telescope!
What's up there way beyond the sky
where planets spin and comets fly?
Are there kids like me?
And all my friends?
With ice cream, bikes and happy grins?
Do they fly kites in cool March winds?
Do they watch bluebirds
hatch in Spring?
Or camp out at night while
crickets sing?
Have pizza and video games?
Count freight cars on a passing train?
Do they have two suns?
Twenty moons?
Find sand crabs on the beach in June?
Galaxies and solar systems!
Constellations!
Lots of planets!
The Milky Way is really cool
and neutron stars are so dynamic!
How DOES the universe exist?

To find answers to all of this…

That's it!

I've got it!

Yes, THAT'S it!…

I'll be an ASTROPHYSICIST!

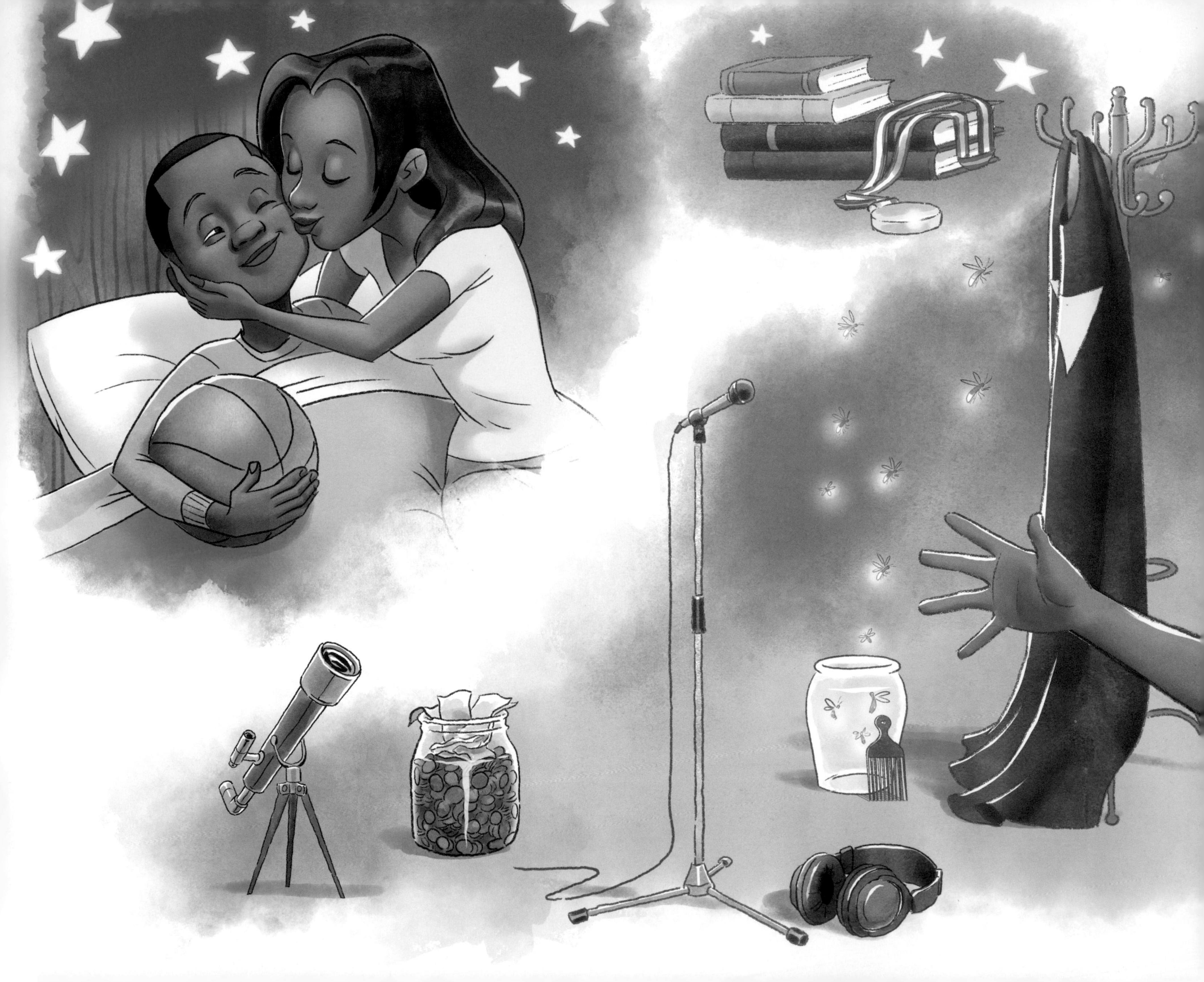

I eat dinner and go to bed,
I watch the stars shine overhead.
Mom repeats the words she said,
"Brilliant is the word to describe
the shine of the stars that make us smile.
Like you—
your smile is brilliant bright.
But now... it's time to say goodnight."
"Be Brilliant," she said softly.
Then two kisses pressed my face.
Like sports cars speeding in my head,
my dreams rev up and race!

GOOD THOUGHTS start
thinking GOOD THINGS—
taking all the sleepy space;
My thoughts are UP...
DOWN... SIDEWAYS,
THINKING all over the place!

I'm SMART and KIND and
HANDSOME, so
There're lots of things I want to know
(while being a SUPERHERO!)
And a LEADER I will be!
I'll build a BUSINESS, too, you'll see;
My family will be proud of me.
I love them, so—
and as I grow, and grow,
and grow... I'll study hard
to make it so!

I'll study hard with all my might,
'cause my future's lookin' mighty bright!

I'll keep learning—there's lot's to know.

Be Brilliant!

That's ME! I'll make it so!

I repeat, and say with joy,

YES!!!...

I'm A BRILLIANT Little Black Boy!

Bbrilliant

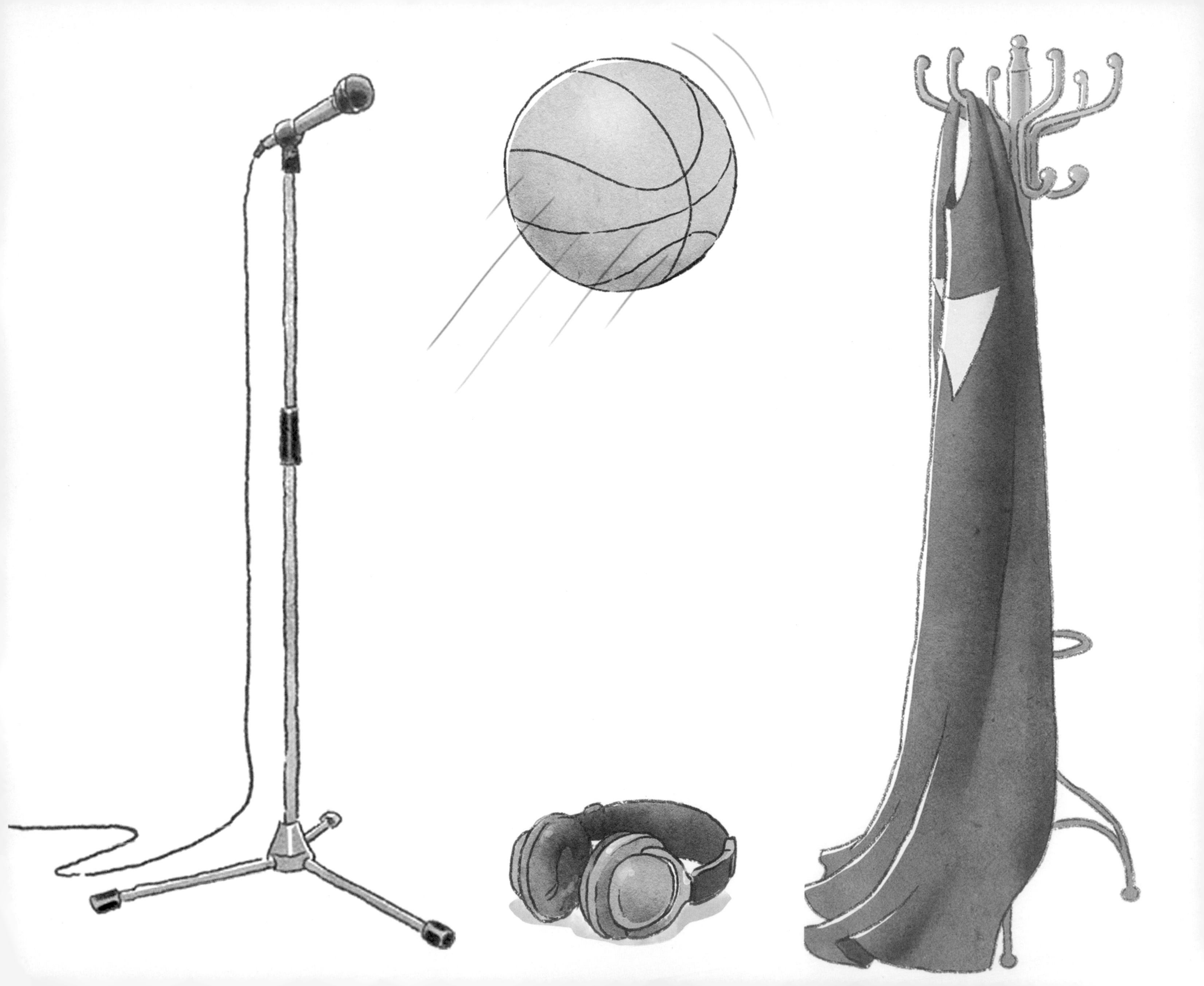

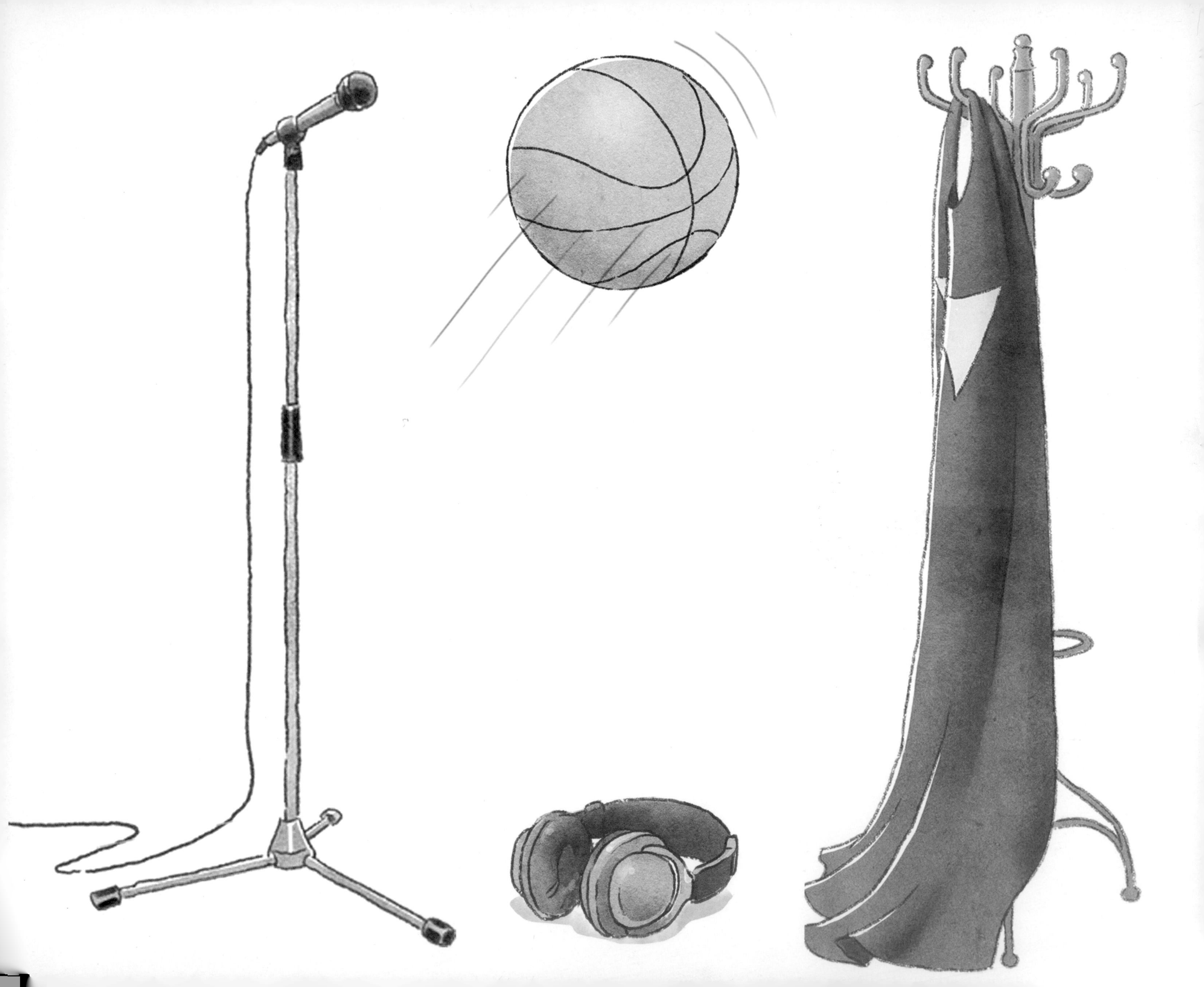